The Bear Did It!

Jan Godfrey
Illustrated by Gunvor Edwards

A TAMARIND BOOK

"Who scribbled on the walls?" asked Mum.
"It wasn't me," said Henry. "The bear did it."
"Which bear?" asked Mum.

"Oh, that bear."

"Who banged the piano very early this morning?"
asked Dad.
"It wasn't me," said Henry. "The bear did it."
"Which bear?" asked Dad.

"Oh, that bear."
That bear again.

"Who muddled up all my socks?" asked Grandpa.
"It wasn't me," said Henry. "The bear did it."
"Which bear?" asked Grandpa.

"Oh, that bear."
That bad bear again.

"Who kicked a ball through my window?"
asked Winston's dad.
"It wasn't me," said Henry. "The bear did it."
"Which bear?" asked Winston's dad.

"Oh, that bear."
That bad, naughty bear again.

"Who opened the gate and let out all my sheep?"
asked Farmer Stringbean.
"It wasn't me," said Henry. "The bear did it."
But Farmer Stringbean said:

"Oh, no, he didn't.
And he didn't shake the apples from my apple tree
and put them in his pocket..."

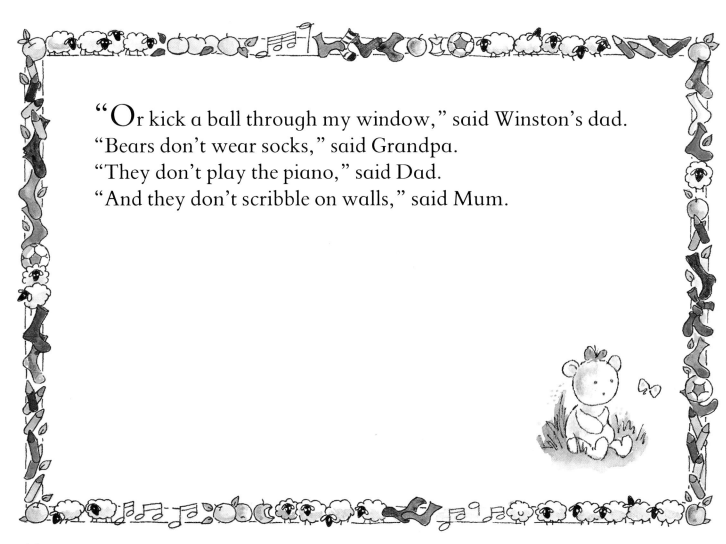

"Or kick a ball through my window," said Winston's dad.
"Bears don't wear socks," said Grandpa.
"They don't play the piano," said Dad.
"And they don't scribble on walls," said Mum.

"Oh, Henry!"

"That bear didn't do all those things at all.
That bear is you.
You've been telling little stories that aren't true.
Look at those apples in your pockets!
Bears don't put apples in their pockets," said Mum.

"Oh, Henry!"

"It's best to tell the truth," said Dad.
"Fancy blaming that poor bear."

"Oh, Henry!"

Henry went very pink all over and hung his head.
Then "HEY!" said Henry.
"Who carried me away with a broom and a cloth
to help clear up the mess?"
And Mum and Dad and Grandpa and Winston's dad
and Farmer Stringbean all laughed and said:

"The bear did it!"

A Tamarind Book
Published in association with SU Publishing
130 City Road, London EC1V 2NJ
ISBN 873824 17 3

First edition 1994

Printed and bound in Singapore